When Worlds Collide

A Journey to the Edge of the Universe
Omsoc and Etnorb—Super Space Cadets

GINO GAMMALDI

Order this book online at www.trafford.com
or email orders@trafford.com

Most Trafford titles are also available at major online book retailers.

© Copyright 2014 Gino Gammaldi.

Illustrations by Peipei

Printed in the United States of America.

ISBN: 978-1-4907-5216-7 (sc)
ISBN: 978-1-4907-5217-4 (hc)
ISBN: 978-1-4907-5218-1 (e)

Library of Congress Control Number: 2014921792

Trafford rev. 12/11/2014

North America & international
toll-free: 1 888 232 4444 (USA & Canada)
fax: 812 355 4082

For my children and grandchildren

Image showing the Athinkobator machine transforming
Cosmo & Bronte into their alter-egos Omsoc & Etnorb.

PROLOGUE

In their last adventure, Cosmo and Bronte led a team of dedicated characters on a quest to discover an important secret. On their journey, they learned how important it was to ask for help and to get the support of others so their search for the secret would succeed.

The Athinkobator machine they discovered was truly a marvelous invention. The people of planet Earth didn't take long to realize the full potential of this scientific marvel. Apart from providing benefits previously unknown to everyone, such as new methods for sustainable agriculture to ensure adequate food for everyone and limitless clean energy resources, Athinkobator managed to do what the human race had failed to achieve throughout its six-billion-year history: It gave all people hope. It abolished poverty. It placed everyone on a level playing field of equality. It instilled in the people of Earth a true sense of well-being for all races. It could achieve almost anything that was of benefit not just to mankind, but also to the inhabitants of other worlds. Its inbuilt synaptic filters prevented it being used for any evil intent.

It's with this machine that these two friends now manage to again take us on a trip. This time, it's a trip beyond our imagination. In this book, they face an enormous challenge—one that transports them to the far reaches of the universe, to worlds of incredible dimensions in star systems yet uncharted.

Five years have passed since their last big adventure. They are both now fifteen years old. During this time, Cosmo and Bronte have been training to become the youngest astronauts that have ever been accepted in the Earth Global Space Program. They are the ones responsible for developing the Athinkobator machine into a scientific marvel that is now capable of doing things never before thought possible.

The capabilities of its central computer are now nothing less than staggering, incorporating bionic as well as linear circuitry. Its processing functions enable direct linkage with all of Earth's computer and robotic systems, which provide a consistent flow of data into its six independent cores. It has become a thinking, self-learning machine that can harness the power of the sun's proton-proton cycle so as to give its central processing unit (CPU) almost limitless capability. With this solar power at their disposal and using the Techtronic Simulator Conversion Capsules fused to Athinkobator's morphosynthesis computer core, Cosmo and Bronte have programmed Athinkobator to metamorphose themselves into the alter egos Omsoc and Etnorb—fearless do-gooders who, at all times, are ready for action. It's simply a matter of entering the Techtronic Simulator Conversion Capsules (TSCC), and Athinkobator does the metamorphosis by irradiating their entire bodies with a carefully programmed particle stream of proton anti-matter. Many times they have been called upon by important people to solve very difficult problems. Their reputation as ambassadors for peace has spread far and wide within the known universe.

They always look forward to new adventures and the opportunity to use the powers of

Athinkobator, not only to transport them to their destinations, but also to help them in achieving their objectives. Each time, they become aware of new, expanded dimensions of this machine's power and how it can be used in times of emergencies to help others. Each time, Athinkobator improves on its abilities because it is a machine capable of learning. Its functions are both biological and electronic. Of course, there is always the risk that anything this powerful could also fall into the wrong hands and be used for evil purposes. To avoid this happening, special security measures have been implemented so that any unlawful tampering with Athinkobator is immediately detected and counter measures are activated. These include a complete shutdown of all Athinkobator's computer systems and access to any data cores via its synaptic filters while simultaneously running a security scan on the would-be intruder.

Warning sirens signal the intrusion and electronic activators seal shut the entire subterranean compound in which Athinkobator and all its access terminals are housed. Although Athinkobator has been of great assistance in putting in place a system of balanced living equality among all of Earth's inhabitants, there will always, unfortunately, exist an element of humanity that will seek to have an advantage over others. This is why Athinkobator must not fall into the wrong hands. As further security, Athinkobator has been programmed to respond only to the commands of Omsoc and Etnorb. Even they have to first undergo a full particle scan, iris scan, and voice recognition aptitude before Athinkobator will allow access to any of its operating systems. This marvel of human ingenuity is considered to be the invention of the millennium and so must be safeguarded at all costs.

ATHINKOBATOR ACTIVATES

The story begins when Cosmo and Bronte complete a test run inside Athinkobator's Techtronic Simulator Conversion Capsules. They have successfully transformed into their alter egos, Omsoc and Etnorb. Their schedule now required them to do some training in the transgalactic simulator. The session was brief as they had already devoted considerable time to this training during the past few weeks. Because of their important rank within the astronaut programme and because they have to be on a constant level of preparedness for any emergency, they have to maintain their piloting expertise at optimum levels. The simulator is directly linked to all Athinkobator functions and can therefore replicate any condition that astronauts could face at any given time and in any quadrant of space. Its visual displays are given in real time and encompass all three dimensions so as to provide an absolutely correct spatial differential that places the pilot in a true-to-life experience. Omsoc and Etnorb decided that a bit of relaxation would be a good thing, and so they decided to start a game of advanced three-dimensional holographic Minecraft with Athinkobator. It's at that moment that a strange hissing sound is heard coming from Athinkobator's main power source. Thinking that it was probably just a minor malfunction and that Athinkobator's self-diagnostic repair functions would locate and repair the problem, they ignored the sound at first and continued with their game. "I don't think it's anything to be worried about" said Omsoc. "I agree" replied Etnorb, "We'll check later to see what's causing the strange sound."

Image showing the Athinkobator machine activating to receiving the first energy beam. This is when Omsoc and Etnorb (as there alter ego characters) hear the strange hissing noises coming from the massive Athinkobator computer while they are playing 3 dimensional holographic Minecraft. The main screen on Athinkobator goes all fuzzy. Lots of flashing lights from the control panel.......... hissing and static lines surround the computer.

It wasn't long before the hissing sounds started again—Omsoc suddenly became concerned when the noise grew louder. The main screen on Athinkobator's panel became fuzzy. He turned to Etnorb and, with some urgency in his voice, said, "I think we had better check this out. There might be something technically wrong with Athinkobator's linear circuitry."

Athinkobator was able to understand voice commands, so Omsoc located the Language Universal Translator (LUT) switch on Athinkobator's control panel and switched it to Voice Recognition processing mode. The LUT is capable of recognizing and translating any language no matter how obscure. To process any translation, the meaning of a text in the original (source) language is fully restored in the target language by the LUT. It interprets and analyzes all the elements in the text and knows how each word influences another. The LUT software always produces quality translations of any alien language. It is equipped with the latest rule-based machine translation technology algorithms. It relies on countless built-in linguistic rules and billions of bilingual dictionaries for each alien language pair. Etnorb took a position at the controls and spoke clearly into Athinkobator's supersensitive voice receiver, "Athinkobator, conduct self-diagnostic of all technical, bionic, and main computer functions, and report."

It only took an instant from when Etnorb's command was received to when the report was given. Athinkobator was equipped with the latest central processing unit (CPU), which was capable of performing billions of tasks at the same time, and so it only took a matter of milliseconds for Athinkobator to acknowledge Etnorb's command and for it to then conduct a thorough diagnostic check of all its functions. "The report is ready for your analysis," came the computerized voice from Athinkobator. The report showed all of Athinkobator's systems functioning perfectly, but as Etnorb and Omsoc watched the graphic display of complicated algorithms or processes on one of the screens, they noticed that there was a glitch in one of the readings. "Athinkobator has conducted a step-by-step problem-solving procedure, as expected," said Etnorb. Athinkobator had done this through a specially established, recursive computational procedure designed to enable it to solve a problem in a finite number of steps. "But, there must be something that Athinkobator could have missed," replied Omsoc. It took the trained eyes of the two super space cadets to notice the cause of the disturbing anomaly. It was in one of the peripheral communication systems located on an observatory on top of Mount Everest. Etnorb directed Athinkobator to focus on the nature of the anomaly and to diagnose further. This time, Etnorb requested that the report be given verbally by Athinkobator so that a finite comparison could be made with the written report already provided. Before Athinkobator could respond to the order given to it by Etnorb, its main screen filled with a host of hieroglyphic images that made absolutely no sense to either Etnorb or to Omsoc. At the same time, Athinkobator issued a warning that something, from an unknown source, was trying to communicate with them. It could offer no information as to the identity or the nature of this communication. "WARNING: Intruder Alert!" Athinkobator issued this message with an urgency in its voice not heard of before by either Omsoc or Etnorb. It shook them from head to toe and their faces became as white as those of a corpse. They both knew that this was something that was quite out of the ordinary and that it demanded their immediate attention.

ALIEN X-MANKANE

In that instant, a massive energy beam came straight out of Athinkobator's three-dimensional, 302-inch 3.25:1 display ratio screen. It was so intense and of such proportions that it completely filled the room in which they were standing.

Omsoc and Etnorb became transfixed by this blast of energy and found themselves unable to move. They then noticed that something very strange was starting to form inside the beam. As the object began to take shape, it became clear to Omsoc and Etnorb that it was beyond any reality that they had previously encountered. The apparition became fully formed within the beam of energy in the shape of a hologram. It had a body that looked like rough stone and was shaped like a long macaroni noodle. There were six spindly tentacle-like around its body, and it had a face that resembled a computer chip. They had never seen anything like this.

Etnorb turned to Omsoc, saying, "Do you think that Athinkobator is combining its sophisticated computer matrix with its bionic components with the objective of making living matter and computer hardware into a singularity?" Omsoc couldn't believe what Etnorb was saying, much less understand it all. "I read something about this kind of thing in a science book at the school library some years ago, but, I thought then that it was just science fiction and something that could only happen in the distant future. When I mentioned it to one of the teachers, I was told that my mind was twisted and that I should concentrate more on books about singing."

"I can't see why Athinkobator would do that without first receiving some instruction to do so from one of us," said Etnorb. "Even though it has advanced learning capabilities, it should not extrapolate any of its developments into any form of reality without receiving our clearance."

Omsoc and Etnorb stared at the creature for quite some time. Neither of them spoke. The creature also looked at them, perhaps trying to establish who was uglier between Omsoc and Etnorb. After what seemed an eternity, the creature spoke in a language that was very foreign to both Omsoc and Etnorb. It sounded like a combination of machine language and obscure Greek etymology. Thanks to Athinkobator activating its built-in Language Universal Translator (LUT), Etnorb and Omsoc were able to understand what this alien being was saying. There was a bit of a delay in aligning the right synchronization of the alien and the English languages, but Athinkobator soon fixed this to ensure proper alignment of the two languages. The creature's voice sounded like it was coming from a long way from where they stood. It also sounded hollow. Nothing had prepared them for this eventuality. In all their past adventures through the vastness of space, this was the first time that they had actually encountered something that seemed to defy all the laws of probability. Yet here it was, staring them in the face in a manner that was bewildering yet not threatening.

"I am X-Mankane," said the creature.

"I come to you from the edge of your known universe with an urgent request for help. My world is called Xulud, an ancient planet ten thousand times the size of your world. The people of my world are the Sebemo, and we are facing a great danger from a race known as the Cyclopzorgs, from the planet Ocat. They have been threatening to change the way we live. We cannot let this happen. My leader, Grayluke, has heard that you are able to solve problems in a way that benefits everyone. It has taken us one thousand of your Earth years to find you. The Cyclopzorgs believe their way of life is better and that all worlds should follow their example. We have never been to their world, but we have seen images sent to our ancestors, by the Cyclopzorgs, many thousands of years ago. They have an animal shape with bear- and giraffe-like features. They do not look friendly. They have visited many other worlds and have succeeded in changing their way of living. As yet, they have not come to our planet, Xulud. However, we do believe that it will only be a matter of time before they do come. When this happens, there is certainly going to be a lot of resistance by my people even though they are not used to fighting. The loss of innocent lives will be enormous. We are very happy with the way things are on our world, and we do not want this to change."

While X-Mankane was explaining the plight of the people on planet Xulud, Omsoc and Etnorb were joined by many high-ranking officials. One of them was a five-star general who came and stood beside Omsoc and Etnorb. "This is highly important with national security implications," he said.

Image of the alien X-Mankane

A massive energy beam comes straight out of Athinkobator's main screen. It is so intense and of such proportions that it completely fills the room in which they are standing. Omsoc and Etnorb become transfixed by this blast of energy and find themselves unable to move. They then notice that something very strange is starting to form inside the beam. It has a body that looks like rough stone and is shaped like a long macaroni noodle. There are six spindly-like tentacles around its body and it has a face that resembles a computer chip; he is representative of the Sebemo race.

ALIEN AGGIE-BUG

As Omsoc and Etnorb were trying to comprehend all of what X-Mankane had said to them, Athinkobator flashed a warning that something else was coming through another of its visual portals. With no time to react, Omsoc and Etnorb were again startled by another huge beam of energy. This one was very colourful and filled with lots of stars and swirls of clouds. The hologram taking shape in this beam of energy was very pretty indeed. She looked almost human, except her head was pointy, and she had wings. She spoke with a soft voice. "Hello," she said, "I am Aggie-Bug. My home world is called Esile, and it is not far from the world of X-Mankane, only two million light years. My people are called the Gubeigga, and I would like to say to you that what X-Mankane is saying is correct. My world is also being threatened by the same race of

Cyclopzorgs. We don't know what to do. The ruler of my world is Queen Becca, who loves her people very much and wants to make sure nothing bad happens to them. Can you also help us?"

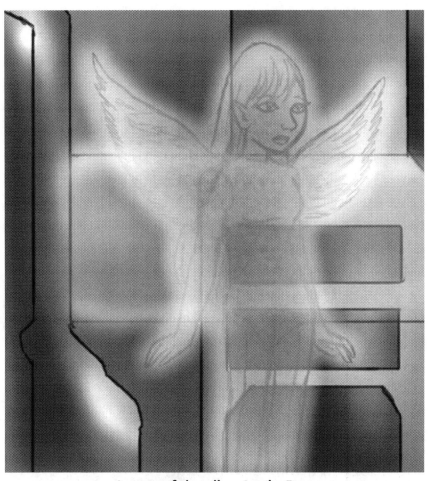

Image of the alien Aggie-Bug

Soon after the arrival of alien X-Mankane, Athinkobator flashes a warning that something else is coming through another of its visual portals. This energy beam is very colourful and filled with lots of stars and swirls of clouds. The hologram taking shape in this beam of energy is very pretty indeed. She looks almost human except her head is pointy and she has wings. She represents the Gubeigga race.

INFORMATION PROCESSING

All this was happening so fast that Omsoc and Etnorb were having difficulty in processing all the information. "Make sure Athinkobator is recording all of this," said Omsoc with a voice that echoed urgency.

"Okay," said Etnorb. Athinkobator's LUT was working in overdrive to translate the languages of the Sebemo and the Gubeigga.

X-Mankane then added, "I have a very capable Sebemo warrior who can formulate an attack on the Cyclopzorgs. His name is Emo-Demo and commands the starship *Kert1701*. We are prepared to fight for our world if you, Omsoc, and you, Etnorb, are prepared to lead us."

Then Aggie-Bug, with some alarm in her voice, said, "I don't think violence is the answer. I also have a capable warrior who can do the same thing. His name is Majac, who commands the super–galaxy starship *JJ57*, which is capable of destroying entire galaxies with its array of quantum fusion solar articulated weaponry. He has also helped to develop a new dimension of avionics, which can be activated directly by the alignment of his own brain wave patterns with his ship's onboard computer. But there must be another way. My queen, Becca, believes Omsoc and Etnorb can come up with a solution that will not lead to fighting between our worlds. We do not want to lose any of our 50 billion Gubbeiga population on our planet, and I'm sure, X-Mankane, your leader, Grayluke, would prefer not to lose any of his 120 billion Sebemos."

Athinkobator took this opportunity to project some images of the starships *Kert1701* and *JJ57* together with their associated fleet of specially equipped warrant-class fighter ships.

"They certainly look formidable indeed," said Etnorb.

"Yes," said Omsoc, "but I agree with Aggie-Bug in that we should find an alternative solution. The use of force ought to be the very last resort."

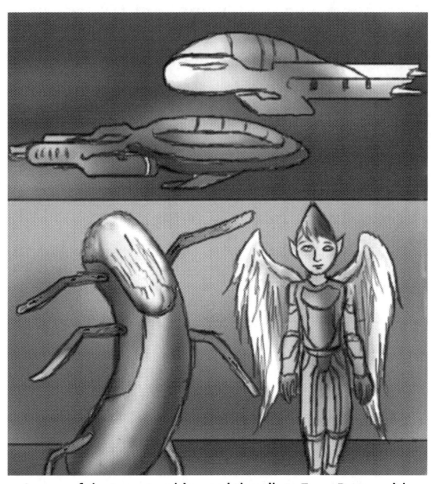

Image of the two starships and the pilots Emo-Demo with starship Kert1701 and Majac with starship JJ57

Emo-Demo looks like X-Mankane (has a body that looks like rough stone and is shaped like a long macaroni noodle. There are six spindly-like tentacles around his body and has a face that resembles a computer chip............the **Sebemo** race).
Majac looks like the alien Aggie-Bug (looks almost human except his head is pointy and he has wings............of course, Aggie-Bug is female and Majac is male. The **Gubbeiga** race).
The starships are capable of destroying entire galaxies with their array of sophisticated weaponry. They will be accompanied by their own fleet of starships later.

Omsoc and Etnorb remained speechless but only for a few moments. They spoke together. It was like they had already rehearsed their answer. "Of course we will help," they said.

They couldn't believe what was happening. This was like a dream come true. To be able to travel across a universe of uncharted space to help two giant worlds attain a peaceful resolution to a conflict that a planet inhabited by the Cyclopzorgs race was threatening. Omsoc and Etnorb were pleased but, at the same time, surprised that their reputation had spread to such limits of the universe. They knew that they could help. But they were diligent enough to realize that this venture into the vast unknown could pose dangers never before experienced. It would be very foolish of them indeed if they did not first ascertain what could be in store for them. Yes, their intentions were admirable, and this was a trait inherent in these two intrepid adventurers, but they knew that they had to be cautious in their approach.

"Let's check with Athinkobator as to how it's processing all of the information it has been recording," said Etnorb.

"Good idea," replied Omsoc. "I'm sure we'll be OK, but it always pays to be careful."

X-Mankane and Aggie-Bug remained in their respective energy beams while Omsoc and Etnorb positioned themselves at Athinkobator's control panel and deactivated the LUT. They did not want X-Mankane and Aggie-Bug to know what they might be planning just yet. They switched Athinkobator to manual control and to report only to their audible frequency and asked it about the possibility of success and what levels of danger they could be facing, knowing that this adventure would stretch their skills to the limit. The five-star general and other officials also gathered around Athinkobator. Everyone was hoping for the best outcome. Athinkobator soon gave them the answers based upon all the information it had so far collected since the appearance of the two aliens. Its computer systems went into hyperdrive as Athinkobator analysed the aliens at a subatomic level and researched their origins, taking into account all aspects of their home worlds. It also conducted an evaluation of Ocat, the Cyclopzorgs' home planet. However, it had some difficulty in establishing the real nature of the inhabitants of this strange planet; something didn't seem quite right and didn't compute effectively within its database of logic algorithms. Athinkobator processed the report and was careful not to create any alarm by admitting a lack of credible information about the inhabitants of planet Ocat.

The verbal report delivered directly to Omsoc and Etnorb, by Athinkobator, was as follows: "The first danger will be travelling to the far distant worlds from which X-Mankane and Aggie-Bug have come. Will you survive the journey? You will be travelling in the same energy beams that brought X-Mankane and Aggie-Bug to planet Earth. These beams are like 'worm holes within worm holes,' and according to my findings, the gravitational stresses inside are so great. They cannot be calculated with any degree of acceptable accuracy. Travel within these will require an almost infinite amount of energy because, at such speeds, objects become infinitely heavier. It is uncertain as to whether my in-built faster-than-light transporter array is powerful enough to create the energy required for such conditions. It has an initial parsec range of 1,500,000 km, at which point the beam would require boosting."

X-Mankane and Aggie-Bug sensed Omsoc's and Etnorb's concern.

X-Mankane was first to speak. "I sense some kind of concern, is there a problem?" Omsoc explained about the huge amount of energy that would be required to enable transport to their destinations. "Do not worry about the possibility of your transporter array's limitations," said X-Mankane. "Our advanced technology for hyperspace transport will be able to provide the boost required at all intervals through the use of our own energy beams, which can link to Athinkobator transporter array to provide all the energy required to get you to any destination." These beams consist of Quaser particle streams that are powerful enough to shift even the positions of objects as dense as neutron stars.

Athinkobator continued, "The next big concern will be the Cyclopzorgs. What kind of a race of creatures are they? Will they be prepared to negotiate an amicable truce with the Sebemos and the Gubeiggas?"

"I am especially concerned about this part," said Omsoc.

"I agree," said Etnorb. "It seems like Athinkobator is concealing something about the real nature of this race. It means that we will need to be extra cautious in our approach when confronting this race of mysterious beings if we are to achieve any level of success with our negotiations."

Athinkobator continued with its verbal reporting directly to Omsoc and Etnorb: "How will you, Omsoc and Etnorb, return to Earth? What amount of Earth time will have passed? Will you return to the present?"

Although Omsoc and Etnorb were not novices when it came to interstellar travel, they were experiencing a bit of trepidation, concern. The location of the planets Xulud and Esile were at the very edge of the known universe in a star system so remote that no journey from Earth to that quadrant had ever been undertaken before. The propulsion capabilities of Earth's starships were not sufficiently sophisticated to allow such dimensions of space to be traversed in any one lifetime. Again, Aggie-Bug and X-Mankane both sensed their concerns. They assured Omsoc and Etnorb that with the technology that the Sebemo and Gubeigga races had developed at their disposal, the never-before-attempted journey was certainly possible. "We will share our technology with you," they both said.

"What we ask from you are your leadership and negotiation skills. Because of the critical nature of what our planets could potentially lose, we cannot compromise our approach to the Cyclopzorgs in any way. Are you willing to come with us? Our people need you."

This opportunity to experience new worlds and at the same time help to build good relations between these worlds was too good to miss. Besides, Omsoc and Etnorb felt it was their civic duty to offer whatever help they could.

"I know that we haven't undertaken such an enormous task before," said Etnorb, "but we have helped a lot of people, not just on our own planet, Earth, but also on many planets in other star systems. We have much experience, and so far, our success rate has been unblemished."

Omsoc pondered for a few minutes on what Etnorb had just said. "You're right again, Etnorb. We have never refused a call for help in the past, and we're not going to start now. Activate Athinkobator's Language Universal Translator (LUT), but link it just to yours and my communicators and to X-Mankane's and Aggie-Bug's receivers."

"Athinkobator," commanded Etnorb, "print out a computer-generated integrated portable visual overlay of all probabilities and destination coordinates."

Athinkobator gave Omsoc and Etnorb a blueprint of a plan to follow, including all grids leading to their projected destinations. This was downloaded into their retractable, handheld, holographic, positronic quark computer pads. The statistical success rate given by Athinkobator was 56.426 percent. This was just a preliminary estimate, which Athinkobator stated could be improved during the actual execution of the project, during which fresh data would be collected, especially on the Cyclopzorg race, to further evaluate the extent of logistical probability. There would be many unknown variables that could affect the final outcome of the project. However, this was not going to deter the great determination of Omsoc and Etnorb. Their resolve was complete and unanimous and would know no bounds. The way of life of two worlds hung in the balance, and the responsibility for bringing about a peaceful resolution to their dilemma was now in their very capable hands. Would they definitely accept the challenge?

Image of Omsoc and Etnorb reviewing their probability of success
They are sitting in front of Athinkobator's main terminal
extrapolating all the available data about what they have been
told by the two aliens (X-Mankane and Aggie-Bug).
Lots of information is appearing on the main screen.
It's in the form of hieroglyphics which Athinkobator
will translate using its Universal Translator Unit.

DECISION TIME

The projection of success given by Athinkobator was good enough for Omsoc and Etnorb. After weighing up the possible levels of danger, they switched the LUT for general communication. They addressed X-Mankane and Aggie-Bug together, saying, "We heard and understood your request for help. We have evaluated the inherent dangers in this venture. We have a plan we think could work. Because you have both come such a long way and because the cause is so worthy, we both agree to offer you our expert services."

X-Mankane and Aggie-Bug were pleased and encouraged by this positive response. They immediately communicated this to their respective leaders on the planets Xulud and Esile. This time, they decided to use Athinkobator's long-range, intergalactic signal-relay system, which is able to communicate at the speed of thought. Instantly and to the great surprise of Omsoc and Etnorb, the leaders of planets Xulud and Esile, Grayluke and Queen Becca, then revealed themselves to Omsoc and Etnorb in the form of holograms so as to thank them personally for their courage and dedication to the pursuit of peace and happiness between the inhabitants of very different worlds. "Thank you," said Grayluke and Queen Becca together. "We are very pleased that you have accepted our commission to be our respective ambassadors on this very important mission. Go with our blessings and our hope for a successful outcome."

Images of Queen Becca & Grayluke

They are the **leaders** of the people on planets Xulud and Esile. In
this image they appear as holograms to Omsoc and to Etnorb.
Again, the planet Xulud is where X-Mankane comes from, so,
his leader will obviously look like him (they look like rough
stone and are shaped like long macaroni noodles. They have
six spindly-like tentacles around their bodies and have faces
that resemble a computer chip; they are the Sebemo race. The
planet Esile is where Aggie-Bug comes from, so, her leader
will obviously look like her (The inhabitants of planet Esile are
quite good looking. They look almost human except that their
heads are pointy and have wings; they are the Gubeigga race.

In a blinding flash of energy, X-Mankane and Aggie-Bug beamed back to their own worlds while Omsoc and Etnorb tried to extract as many details as they could about the Cyclopzorg race. Athinkobator has a vast database of information on practically every alien race that exists in the known universe. Although at first it had not been able to properly ascertain the exact nature of the Cyclopzorg race, its central computer had been constantly searching for more clues since the first report had been made available to Omsoc and Etnorb. It now was able to show Omsoc and Etnorb some preliminary images of the Cyclopzorgs.

As these were flashed onto Athinkobator's huge screen, the look of disbelief that came upon Omsoc and Etnorb was nothing less than staggering. Nothing had prepared them for how these alien beings were portrayed. If these images were in any way representative of this race, then it was clear as to why the Sebemos and Gubeigga races felt intimidated.

"They are so huge," said Etnorb.

They had features that resembled a combination of brown bear and giraffe and had a large eye protruding from their stomach. They carried strange weapons that seemed to have enormous destructive power and lived in huge ice caves that dwarfed every other piece of landscape that surrounded them. Their planet was even bigger than the planets of the Sebemo and Gubeigga races combined and was mostly covered in ice, huge mountains, and oceans the colour of green jelly.

"It looks like a dark and hostile world," said Omsoc.

They both wondered how life, as they knew it, could even exist there. From the information given to them by X-Mankane and Aggie-Bug, they knew that the Cyclopzorgs were a race that, for billions of years, had been trying to convert the way of life of the Sebemo and Gubeigga races to be the same as their own.

"It's easy to see how any race would be easily intimidated by the Cyclopzorgs," said Etnorb. "They look so fierce."

Apparently, they were a race that felt they had to try to assimilate all inhabitants of other worlds into accepting their type of existence without compromise. Theirs was a culture of domination, of assimilation. They had already achieved this manipulation and conversion of cultures on some other planets. The reported results of this bullying method had been less than satisfactory for the inhabitants of those worlds. The situation had now reached the point in which the Cyclopzorgs were prepared to use force on the inhabitants of Xulud and Esile. But would it end there? Would Earth ultimately be facing the same threat from these perpetrators of disharmony? Omsoc and Etnorb realized they had no choice but to act now before it was too late for Xulud and Esile and, perhaps, in time, even for planet Earth itself.

THE JOURNEY STARTS

The information Athinkobator provided was very disturbing to Omsoc and Etnorb.

"We have to do everything possible to ensure success," said Omsoc.

"I'll check with Athinkobator as to the preparations needed for the journey," said Etnorb. "Given that we have to travel through the wormhole that will be created by Athinkobator and boosted by the energy provided by X-Mankane's and Aggie-Bug's technologies, we need to establish the coordinates of both the planet Xulud and the planet Esile." "I know," said Omsoc. "We have the blueprint of Athinkobator's computer-generated overlay plan. Let's put on our multi-atmospheric space suits as created by Athinkobator's sophisticated matter replicators." As they were preparing themselves, Etnorb made a very important observation. "One thing that we must be very sure about is that we must not appear to be threatening in any way to any of the Sebemo, Gubeigga, or Cyclopzorg races. We must remain neutral. Therefore, there must be no weapons carried in this quest for peace between the planets." Omsoc nodded in agreement. "You're right," he said. "I know I am. But, I don't mind admitting that I feel somewhat vulnerable without any weapons," said Etnorb in a shaky voice. "I am confident in the fact that Athinkobator is capable of providing any range of weaponry that we might require and which could provide us with any defence capability that could be required for when we meet with the Cyclopzorgs,"replied Omsoc."

"We need to understand that this is to be a mission of peace, Etnorb. I do understand your concerns for our safety, but, we are well trained in what we are about to do. Besides, Athinkobator will be watching our every move."

Omsoc and Etnorb were acting as ambassadors for two worlds that wished to protect their idyllic lifestyle, one that they had developed over eons of time. These two worlds had eliminated any need for greed or rivalry. Everyone on these two planets was given equality even for their most basic needs. The sole aim of the leaders of these two worlds was to maintain what they had achieved and even to improve and to share the well-being of their people. They had become great thinkers and had made incredible progress in the fields of science and technology such that it was millions of years ahead of Earth.

"We musn't forget, Omsoc, that the Cyclopzorgs are also very advanced in all fields of progress and that their intentions are not as benign as those of the Sebemo and Gubeigga races."

"Yeah, I know this," replied Omsoc. "I know that their motive is to be supreme rulers of the universe and all its star systems. To this end, they are probably prepared to use whatever means is required to achieve this aim. However, our approach has to be seen as being a peaceful one. Otherwise, we will lose any advantage that we might have."

"Omsoc, I have the blueprint of our plan as developed by Athinkobator. It shows that you are to go to the planet Xulud, and I am to go to the planet Esile."

"Yes," said Omsoc. "I see that once there, we will each talk with the respective leaders so as to establish what should be done to get the Cyclopzorg race to be on friendly terms with each of these planets." The blueprint also clearly showed that on their journey, the plan was to stop at a planet called Barbabeetle.

"Remember the deep research with Athinkobator that we did, when we asked it to give us some projections for our expected success rate? Well, that's why this planet called Barbabeetle appears on the blueprint of our journey. I believe that Athinkobator has established that on this planet lives a race that has never experienced any conflict or any differences with any of its many neighbouring worlds." Etnorb kept studying the blueprint.

Sure enough, when Omsoc checked this, it showed that this race had evolved over hundreds of billions of years into beings that resembled beautiful sunflowers. Similar to the inhabitants of Xulud and Esile, they were great thinkers who had outgrown greed and violence of any kind. The one main difference was that they had not and were unlikely to be faced with any unwarranted onslaught by the likes of the dictatorial Cyclopzorgs. This race was known as the Brainoids. They had a reputation as advisors and humanitarians. They welcomed all races to their world—a world that was protected against any would-be assailants by an extraordinary array of force fields. These force fields also incorporated cloaking technology that made the whole planet invisible when under any threat.

"Look at this," said Omsoc as he checked Athinkobator's computer-generated overlay plan. "This planet can also shift its orbit and rotation parameters by distorting the space surrounding it so that its grid location will be almost impossible to calculate." That was a correct observation by Omsoc.

Image of the planet Barbabeetle

The planet's orbital trajectory can be shifted within a time and space continuum that transcends all known mathematical probability. The planet can position itself in any star system. This offers the inhabitants of this planet great protection. Planet Barbabeetle gives the illusion of a planet transposed with another planet. It is like two worlds in one. One world appears very sinister while the other appears peaceful

The planet's orbital trajectory could be shifted within a time and space continuum that transcended all known mathematical probability. The planet could position itself in any star system. This offered the inhabitants of this planet great protection. It took the complex computing power of Athinkobator to discover this unique world and to include it on the journey that they were about to embark upon.

"Not only that," continued Omsoc, "but I think that there is even more to this world than we are led to believe." Etnorb examined the computer overlay of the planet's surface more intensely on the Quark Computer Pad, and what he discovered was even more fantastic. Planet Barbabeetle gave the illusion of a planet transposed with another planet. It was like two worlds in one. One world appeared very sinister while the other was peaceful. The Brainoids could project whichever image of their world that they deemed appropriate, depending on the nature or intent of the alien race approaching its orbit. This was truly an amazing planet. Athinkobator determined that Omsoc and Etnorb could use all the help they could get so as to give them every advantage as ambassadors for peace, considering the high level of importance of the task they were undertaking.

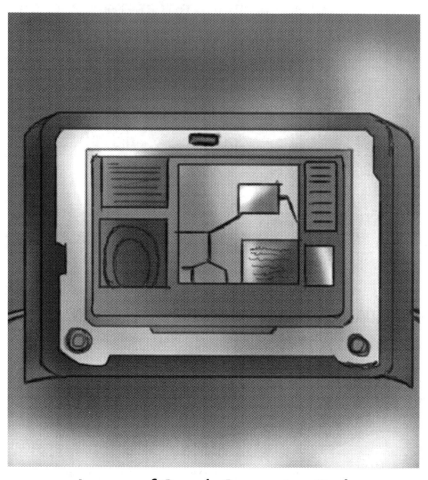

<u>Image of Quark Computer Pad</u>
Image of a highly sophisticated piece of electronic equipment vital for language translation and for situation and logistical analysis. It has a flexible screen which rolls up like a newspaper. Shows virtual planetary topography in real time.

THE BRAINOIDS

Omsoc and Etnorb agreed with Athinkobator's deductions regarding the interim visit to planet Barbabeetle.

"I'm looking forward to meeting the leaders of this unusual world to see if they would be prepared to help the inhabitants of Xulud and Esile," said Etnorb.

"Because of their vast experience in humanitarian matters, I'm sure that they will be able to offer us some strategy that will help us in convincing the Cyclopzorgs to accept that each of the people on those planets has a right to live on their own world in the manner in which they are accustomed to living. What we certainly need is some expert guidance as to the best way to negotiate with the Cyclopzorgs leader."

All was ready. Omsoc and Etnorb sent a signal to X-Mankane and Aggie-Bug simultaneously to inform them they were ready for their journey. Both X-Mankane and Aggie-Bug were quick to respond from their respective home planets, to which they had transported earlier through their high-intensity energy beams. They signaled their top flight warrior commanders, Emo-Demo and Majac, who immediately boarded their intergalactic starships capable of wormhole transport through curved space. This meant they could travel vast distances, measurable only in light-year terms, almost instantly. They had just returned from a mission to a distant asteroid which had huge deposits of a substance called Oilgig. This stuff was rich in properties that both the planets of Xulud and Esile needed to sustain their energy requirements. Emo-Demo and Majac had accompanied a scientific expedition sent to determine the mining possibilities on the asteroid. They arrived on Earth, materializing through Athinkobator's plasma-diotic porthole right outside the secret underground compound from which Omsoc and Etnorb conducted all their operations.

"There is no time to waste," said Omsoc.

The two intrepid travelers had already been briefed by Athinkobator and had suited up. Because their journey was to be in starships designed to sustain life forms very different to themselves, special space gear had to be developed, which would provide them with all the right life-support systems simulating Earth conditions. This had required considerable research by Athinkobator, taking into consideration the environmental conditions on the starships, the G forces of faster-than-light speed motion, and the impact this might have on Omsoc and Etnorb's Earth-like physiology.

"I'll be travelling with Emo-Demo in his *Kert1701* starship," said Omsoc.

"I'll be with Majac in his *JJ57* starship," said Etnorb while checking to make sure that they both had not forgotten to pack their retractable, portable, holographic-display positronic-quark computer pads. These highly sophisticated pieces of electronic equipment were vital for language translation and for situation and logistical analysis. They were to be simply passengers during the journey. Their pilots would get them to where they had to go.

"I'm really looking forward to getting underway," said Etnorb. "I think that we are as prepared as we can be. But even if we're not, I believe that we have sufficient backup resources to assist us with the massive computing power of Athinkobator on our side."

"Yes," said Omsoc. "But don't forget that we are also enlisting the help of the leader of the planet Barbabeetle."

Omsoc and Etnorb were now very confident that with all this help, together with their relentless determination to succeed, a peaceful resolution to the tension among the planets Xulud, Esile, and Ocat would result. Once commanders Emo-Demo and Majac had programmed the coordinates of the peaceful planet Barbabeetle, their onboard computers took overall travel operations. The two starships would travel in tandem, locked within the infinitely powerful forces of the wormhole.

They arrived in a flash of brilliant light. Looking at the onboard chronometers, Omsoc and Etnorb noticed something very odd. Only seconds of ship time had elapsed. However, time on planet Earth had moved on 1,426 years. Because of the curvature of space and travelling at twenty-two thousand times the speed of light, time on board the starships had slowed down in considerable proportions compared to Earth time. "It has suddenly dawned on me," said Omsoc, "that all the people that we have ever known on Earth have died since we started on this trip." Etnorb thought about what Omsoc had just said and hesitated before answering.

"You're right, but I find it hard to understand what has just happened. For everyone living on Earth, 1,426 Earth years has elapsed. For us, it has been just seconds. Are they really all gone? Does anyone now even know that we have embarked on this important assignment? Have we been forgotten?" Their minds reeled at the thought of this amazing phenomena. Omsoc had no answers to Etnorb's very valid questions.

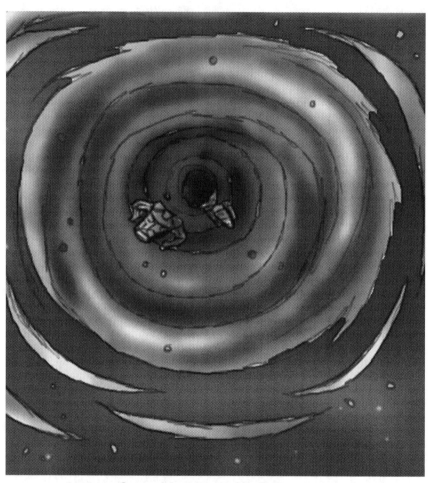

Image of starships emerging from wormhole
Image shows two sleek starships emerging from
a wormhole ...the starships are powerful....the
names of the starships are Kert1701and JJ57

The two galactic ships emerged from the wormhole, as if by magic, and landed on the planet Barbabeetle. They disembarked almost at the entrance of a complex array of glass-like buildings that seemed to reach above the clouds. Each of these buildings was taller than the next. Seeing the look of awe on the faces of their passengers, Commander Majac thought that some explanation might be necessary about the massive buildings.

"The buildings are tall because the area of habitable land mass on this planet is limited," he said. "Therefore, living areas are concentrated where it's most convenient for all inhabitants."

Omsoc and Etnorb marvelled at all that they were seeing.

"That's just part of it," added Emo-Demo. "The tallest of the structures reaches beyond the planet's exosphere and links itself with an orbiting space station so immense that it casts a shadow on the planet. This happens when its alignment with its very luminous, powerful, and energetic quasar cluster is at its optimum position. The space station is an engineering marvel. It is used by the inhabitants of Barbabeetle not just for scientific research and maintaining planet security but also as a recreational facility." This unusual fact was mind-boggling to both Omsoc and Etnorb.

"There is no better place to go for a bit of R & R," said Majac.

Their journey was just beginning, and they wondered what other intriguing and mind-blowing scientific marvels were yet to be revealed to them. Their two pilots seemed to know quite a bit about this sector of space, and Omsoc and Etnorb were grateful that they had been given such knowledgeable and experienced pilots for their very important assignment.

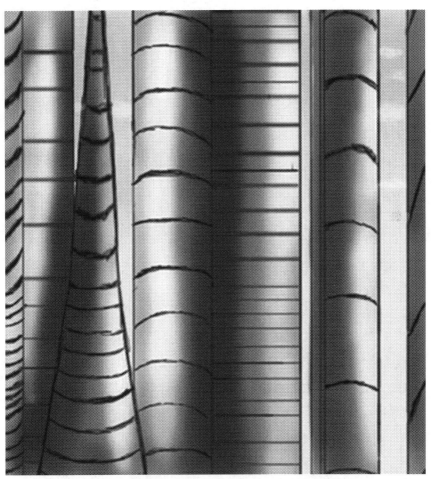

Image of very tall glass buildings on planet Barbabeetle
They disembarked on the planet Barbabeetle almost
at the entrance of a complex array of glass-like
buildings that seemed to reach above the clouds.
Each of these buildings was taller than the next.

It was in the tallest of these buildings that flight commanders Emo-Demo and Majac escorted Omsoc and Etnorb to meet with the supreme ruler of Barbabeetle. Beside the main entrance was the express transport elevator that was programmed to take its carefully screened passengers directly to the uppermost section of the immense building.

"How far up the building do we have to go?" asked Etnorb.

"We need to arrive at the section just below the actual part of the building connecting with the orbiting space station," said Majac.

The elevator was designed to travel on electromagnetic guide rails along the outside of the glass tower. It also was of completely glass construction, allowing an unsurpassed 180-degree lateral view and 360-degree vertical view of its surroundings.

Omsoc and Etnorb realized that they were going to have to keep any feelings of vertigo very much under control as they travelled inside this glass tube. It would be precarious, but they were assured by their starship commanders that there had never been an unsafe incident.

"Just to be sure, we'll check in with Athinkobator through our handheld positronic-quark computer pads," said Omsoc and Etnorb.

A response came instantly from Athinkobator, who had been monitoring their every move since leaving Earth. Their safety was confirmed. As their distance from the ground increased, they began to see the curvature of this unusual planet, then the changing atmospheric conditions, then empty space itself until they arrived at their destination at the entrance to the part of the tower just below the space station. Looking up, the space station covered Omsoc's and Etnorb's entire view of space in a way that numbed their senses.

Image of Space Elevator on planet Barbabeetle
Illustration shows the tallest building reaching a massive space station in orbit around the planet.
It extends from the planet's surface to the
giant space station; like an elevator.

"This thing really is enormous," said Omsoc. "They must be a very advanced race that lives on this planet to be able to build something so big and complex in space."

They entered the building and were led by commanders Emo-Demo and Majac in the direction of a bright light, which fluctuated in intensity and colour. It was like a kaleidoscope that refracted light in varying dimensions and seemingly defying the laws of the physical spectrum.

"You will be meeting with Onigiul, the leader of this planet," said Commander Majac. "He is a very important person. Be respectful at all times."

"We will be," said Etnorb. "Thank you for everything so far."

At this point, commanders Emo-Demo and Majac abruptly separated themselves from Omsoc and Etnorb, who stood motionless.

"I think we are expected to continue towards the light," said Omsoc.

"Look over there!" yelled Etnorb. Along the vast passageways were rows upon rows of sunflower-like people all standing at attention like well-trained soldiers. They were something to behold.

"There must be thousands of them," continued Etnorb as they slowly made their way forward, passing many rooms filled with the sunflower people, who were all engaged in various activities.

Image of the Brainoid people
Illustration shows this race as looking like beautiful sunflowers but with faces that have some human like characteristics

"These must be the Brainoids," said Omsoc. "I think it might be a good idea at this point to send a subspace message to the planets Xulud and Esile. We should let the leaders know that we have arrived safely at planet Barbabeetle and are about to meet with the leader."

Etnorb activated their handheld positronic quark computer pads and punched in the long-range sensor array configuration. Their signal was received simultaneously by both planets. Grayluke appeared on Omsoc's screen, and Queen Becca appeared on Etnorb's screen.

"We are on planet Barbabeetle," reported Omsoc and Etnorb together. "We are about to meet with the leader. We want you to know that we have great confidence and believe that all will go well." They then signed off their communicators.

ONIGIUL

I t was in the biggest of the rooms where Omsoc and Etnorb came face-to-face with Onigiul, the leader of the Brainoid people. He was the biggest sunflower of them all and was standing in the centre of the great hall surrounded by Brainoids who were all nodding to one another and with arms uplifted towards Onigiul. It was a beautiful scene—one that gave Omsoc and Etnorb real conviction that they had come to the right place for some guidance on how to handle the Cyclopzorgs. There was serenity all around them, and soothing humming could be heard permeating the entire area in which they were standing.

"I've never seen anything like this in all my travels through the universe," said Omsoc. "Who would have thought that such creatures could exist?"

"I know what you mean," said Etnorb, "but don't be too surprised. We have both been on many adventures together and have seen things that didn't seem possible before on remote planets."

Omsoc was still admiring all that surrounded them. "Yes, but nothing like this," said Omsoc.

Onigiul turned towards them and gestured to certain Brainoids to move in closer. They moved in unison as if motivated by one controlling entity. "They behave like a collective linked to one mind," whispered Omsoc to Etnorb.

Image of ONIGIUL the leader of the Brainoid race
Onigiul standing in the centre of a large room surrounded by the sunflower people with arms upstretched. Onigiul is the biggest sunflower.

"What do we do now?" wondered Etnorb. They waited to be summoned.

"Come and stand beside me," asked Onigiul. "Look up. I want you to look high up towards the furthermost reaches of the building in which we are standing."

It was then that Omsoc and Etnorb saw something they would never have imagined. A vision of planets and galaxies all in a cluster and surrounded by brilliant light and coloured gases. Suddenly, all the walls in the room disappeared, and it seemed as though they were teetering on the very edge of the universe itself. Omsoc and Etnorb almost went into free fall as they marveled at all that surrounded them—the vision of myriad galaxies all in congruent harmony with one another and bursting with vibrant energy and power. It was easy to see how advanced the technology of the Brainoids was. This planet really could place itself in any quadrant of space.

Image of Omsoc and Etnorb standing alone and in awe of their surroundings

They are standing as if on an edge of space itself
surrounded by distant galaxies. There are planets in
orbit. They are almost teetering on the edge of the
universe itself and marveling at all that they see.

"Listen carefully," said Onigiul as the room returned to normal. It took a little while for Omsoc and Etnorb to regain their equilibrium.

"What now?" said Etnorb.

"Keep quiet," replied Omsoc. "We are in no position to question anything at this stage. All we can do is wait and see what happens."

A voice like no other then filled all the space around them. It was mysterious but sounded full of wisdom. Omsoc and Etnorb became confused.

"Do not be afraid," said Onigiul gently. "Listen carefully, for this is the voice of Ecarg that you are hearing. This is the one who, over eons of time, united all the races of the neighbouring star systems and brought harmony to everyone. Ecarg is the immortal one—the one who lives forever and knows all."

With the voice of Ecarg still ringing in their ears, Etnorb looked at Omsoc and remarked, "We were right to accept Athinkobator's direction on this stopover on this planet Barbabeetle. I am very keen to hear what Ecarg has to tell us."

"So am I," replied Omsoc.

"Yes, you came to the right place," said Onigiul. "Here you will gain the knowledge necessary for you to be able to help the Sebemo and the Gubeigga races. Here you will find a way to make the Cyclopzorgs respect the Sebemo and Gubeigga way of life."

Omsoc and Etnorb listened to what Onigiul was saying.

"We are willing to hear what Ecarg has to say," said Omsoc. "We will always acknowledge the wisdom and the experience of anyone who is willing to share a way that will help others."

Etnorb nodded in agreement and added, "We must be as well prepared as possible. The Sebemo and Gubeigga people are counting on us to succeed in ensuring that their way of life is retained."

ECARG

Although Omsoc and Etnorb could not see Ecarg, they certainly could feel that her presence was very close. Ecarg spoke with these words of wisdom. She spoke gently and slowly so that the two visitors would not be confused in any way. The language spoken by the Brainoid race was nothing that either Omsoc or Etnorb could understand. But Athinkobator's Language Universal Translator (LUT) was used to convert the Brainoid language into English.

"You are travelers from a distant planet called Earth," said Ecarg. "I have been observing your planet for thousands of years. This is the first time I have seen anyone from your planet show a real interest in helping a race alien to themselves. This now gives me a good feeling about Earth people. For too long I have seen your race fighting against themselves to serve their own individual greed for power. Earth people against Earth people, nation against nation. This antagonism against one's own people never serves any good purpose. Over eons of time, the Brainoid race has experienced similar problems amongst its own kind, and we have seen how power corrupts. But we have learned to change our ways. We have accepted the rights of everyone to live in peace and without the threat of poverty. We have evolved from simply relying on amassing material possessions into a race that is caring and understanding—one that has good values and tries to share these good values not only with everyone on our planet but also with inhabitants of other worlds who seek our help."

Omsoc and Etnorb listened to every word. It was like they were in a time warp in which nothing else mattered except for the voice of the wise Ecarg. No other sound could be heard. No other thought seemed possible. Their attention was fixed. Ecarg continued. "You want to know how to help the inhabitants of Xulud and of Esile, don't you?"

"Yes, we do," said Omsoc and Etnorb together.

"Well, you have already made a good start by showing an interest in their problem. What you have to do now is to explain to both the Sebemos and the Gubeiggas how you are going to get the inhabitants of Ocat, the Cyclopzorgs, to understand how important it is that they be allowed to live their own lives as they wish. Is that clear?"

"Yes," replied Omsoc and Etnorb.

"Good . . . this is what you must do." Omsoc and Etnorb waited for the words of wisdom. "Tell the Sebemo and Gubeigga people that how they choose to live their lives is important and that they must always believe this. They must believe in themselves too and not let anyone say they must do things a different way simply because they think their way is better. Everyone should have the right to be free to do what they wish as long as it is within the law and does not hurt anyone else. Every race should be the master of its own destiny, as should every individual."

Omsoc and Etnorb had maintained a link with Athinkobator all the time, and through this link, everything that Ecarg said was being recorded. They didn't want to make any mistakes.

"I learned to value many things throughout my long life," said Ecarg. "But two of the most important things I have learned to value are freedom and time. They are both precious. Freedom is never really appreciated until it is taken away by someone else. The threat of this happening to the Sebemo and Gubeigga races has rightly posed great concerns for them. It is unfortunate that someone is always dying somewhere for what they believe. These two races are obviously proud of who they are and what their heritage represents to them and to their descendants. They are now well aware of what they have and what they stand to lose. Time is irreplaceable; a second lost is a second wasted and can never be retrieved. Time isn't something that is out there, intangible, and unrelated to everyday life. It is life. That's the biggest reason why time is the most important asset to most races. Everything you want to do, see, feel, touch, and experience can only happen within the time that one is given. Everyone must value the freedom they enjoy and the time they have to do so."

Omsoc looked at Etnorb. "Can you see what's happening here? It's all about what people believe and what is right for them. This is exactly the philosophy of beliefs that we are trying to preserve for the Sebemo and Gubeigga races."

Etnorb agreed.

"Once you have talked with the Sebemos and the Gubeiggas," said Ecarg, "go to the planet Ocat and convince the Cyclopzorgs that every race has the right to determine how they should structure their own lives. This is the right of every form of intelligence. Explain to them how much better it would be for them if they allowed the people of the other planets to be themselves and to perhaps share willingly in their different cultures." This made a lot of sense to Omsoc and Etnorb. "The benefits to the Cyclopzorgs could be many. Everyone has something different to offer, and when all of this is brought together, the enrichment gained by all inhabitants of each planet will be enormous. Show them that there is greater reward in giving than there is in taking. Use my world of Barbabeetle and how we live as an example. Let them know that our world is also open to them if they wish to benefit from our experience. Go now and do good for everyone. Believe that you can find beauty anywhere, even in the face of despair and the threat of adversity."

Image of Ecarg
Ecarg as a bright orb of light shining down on Onigiul, Omsoc and Etnorb. She is all knowledgeable. Onigiul is the leader of the Brainoids. He is a big, regal sunflower-like person. Ecarg can only be seen as the brightest of all orbs; something like the sun with beautiful flames surrounding her.

THE SEBEMOS AND THE GUBEIGGAS

Omsoc and Etnorb were very grateful to Ecarg for all her help. They wasted no time in joining Emo-Demo and Majac on their starships.

"I'm still trying to come to grips with all that has happened," said Etnorb.

"That Onigiul is quite a cool dude, and Ecarg certainly knows her stuff," replied Omsoc.

The starships were soon back in the wormhole and preparing their way to the planets Xulud and Esile, where Omsoc and Etnorb would explain to the people how they would convince the Cyclopzorgs to become better neighbours. Time was now of the essence, and so the starship pilots immediately engaged their plasma engines, which used light itself as the propulsion, and set their coordinates for their respective home planets. Billions of kilometers of uncharted space had to be traversed in order to reach their destinations. During this time, Athinkobator was processing all the information that had been recorded during the meeting with Ecarg. This was then relayed into the handheld positronic-quark computer pads of Omsoc and Etnorb. Armed with all this newly acquired knowledge, they knew that they were now well prepared to be real ambassadors for the cause of righteousness. "Ecarg of the Brainoid race was wise indeed and has provided much-needed guidance," said Etnorb, scanning the quark computer pad.

Again, because of the curvature of space and the space distortion created by their plasma engines, the starships reached the planets in just seconds of ship time.

Omsoc was on the planet Xulud, and Etnorb was on the planet Esile. They approached each of the leaders (Grayluke and Queen Becca) and did exactly as the wise Ecarg had instructed them to do. An intergalactic, subspace video link was established between the two planets so that what

Omsoc and Etnorb were saying was delivered, heard, and seen at the same time by both the Sebemo and Gubeigga leaders. They were very encouraged by all this, and so they decided to tell all their people how Omsoc and Etnorb were going to be their ambassadors in appealing to the Cyclopzorgs. Before doing so, they summoned their two most important representatives, X-Mankane and Aggie-Bug, to attend an immediate video conference between the two worlds. X-Mankane sat with the leader of Xulud, Grayluke, and Aggie-Bug sat with the leader of Esile, Queen Becca. They could all see each other and communicate through huge screens, which projected them as holographic images across the trillions of space kilometers. Grayluke and Queen Becca greeted each other again.

"I'm so very pleased that we were able to find the planet Earth and to be able to engage the services of Omsoc and Etnorb," said Aggie-Bug.

"I know," added X-Mankane.

"I wasn't sure at first as to whether we had approached the right ones to intervene with the Cyclopzorgs on our behalf. But now I know that we made the right choice. X-Mankane, do you agree that we have made the right choice?"

X-Mankane answered without hesitation. "I certainly believe that we have. It's now up to them to prove what they can do."

This is true, thought Aggie-Bug. *It is now up to them.*

"Our way of life is now in the hands of two very capable people," said Aggie-Bug. "We must have faith."

Both X-Mankane and Aggie-Bug then fell silent as they waited for their respective leaders to make comment. Grayluke and Queen Becca again turned their attention to each other. "I do not think we have anything to fear," said Queen Becca, addressing Grayluke.

"You're right," replied Grayluke. "Besides, we have no other alternative, unless we decide to give in to the Cyclopzorgs."

Quickly Aggie-Bug interjected, "No no no. We cannot let this happen. We've all seen how grotesque and dominating the Cyclopzorgs are.

We cannot and should not allow them to rule over our planets."

Without prompting, X-Mankane added, "I couldn't agree more with Aggie-Bug. Although we haven't physically seen the Cyclopzorgs, thank the stars for that, we have seen all the evidence of their power and determination to force their way of life on all races."

"Yes," said Aggie-Bug, "there is an entire archive of video images and more on each of our planets, all of which portray them as tyrants—absolute, tyrannical rulers who just want to have authority over others."

The two leaders held X-Mankane and Aggie-Bug in very high esteem and sincerely wanted to assure them that they each had made the right decision by selecting Omsoc and Etnorb.

"Have no fear," said Grayluke. "Queen Becca and I are very confident in the ability of Omsoc and Etnorb to deliver what they have promised."

This was good enough for both X-Mankane and Aggie-Bug. During this video conferencing between the two planets, Omsoc and Etnorb sat quietly, listening to the exchange of words and feelings—Omsoc in the room with the leader of the Sebemo race, and X-Mankane on planet Xulud, while Etnorb sat with the leader of the Gubeigga race and Aggie-Bug.

"Let's now tell all our people," said Queen Becca to Grayluke. They did this from where they sat using the very sophisticated video system that could cut into all the two planets' broadcasts. The people cheered happily.

"Time for us to embark," said Omsoc. "Our starships are fueled and ready to go." Once on board, they spent some time with the two pilots, commanders Emo-Demo and Majac, discussing the route the starships were to take. This time, both were heading to the distant planet of Ocat at the edge of the known universe. Their intention was clear, as was their destination. Their hope was that they would succeed on behalf of the Sebemos and the Gubeiggas. There was much at stake for them.

Images of Sebemo and Gubeigga leaders
This image shows the leaders (Grayluke & Queen Becca). They are on their own planets and each is being viewed by their own race via a huge screen. The two images are on separate planets. Etnorb and Omsoc observe all communications.

PLANET OCAT

Commanders Emo-Demo and Majac both locked in the same coordinates as the starships entered the wormhole for the third time. Again, because of the physics of curved space, only seconds passed, and they were in orbit around the planet Ocat, a planet so large that its gravitational pull was almost as severe as that of a black hole. It took all of commanders Emo-Demo's and Majac's piloting skills to manoeuvre their starships into a safe orbit and then land them safely. This complex manoeuvre was only made possible with the assistance of Athinkobator's vast computer power and high-energy proton-proton charged particle beam, which helped to control the steep trajectory that the starships had to navigate. It was a bumpy ride. "I don't care too much about repeating that experience," said Etnorb.

This was a dark, icy world—a world besieged by constant and severe magnetic storms and tectonic plate activity. Its surface was very inhospitable, and Omsoc and Etnorb became a bit fearful to step out of the starships.

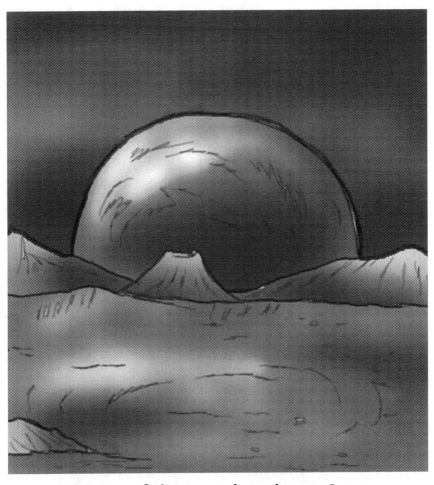

<u>Image of the massive planet Ocat</u>
A dark, icy world, with heavy storm and volcanic
activity.

Then a signal came to them from Athinkobator across the trillions of light years. With the newly installed communication software that Athinkobator had developed, it was able to send signals anywhere without any delay between transmission and receiving time. The signal said, "Omsoc and Etnorb, I see you have arrived safely on the planet Ocat. I know that it is unsafe to leave your starships. Using my matter disintegrator and reintegrator atomic particle beam, I can dematerialize you and then project and rematerialize you anywhere on the planet. All I need is the coordinates of where you wish to go."

Omsoc and Etnorb listened. They weren't too sure. "I don't know about this new technology developed by Athinkobator," said Omsoc. "It's never been tried before." But they really did not have much choice.

"I think we have to go with it," said Etnorb. "I certainly don't fancy making my way through that rotten storm activity that seems to be ravaging this planet." Throwing caution to the wind, they immediately relayed their destination coordinates to Athinkobator. "Here goes nothing," said Omsoc as the switch was thrown. Instantly, their entire bodies felt like they were dissolving into thin air as they were converted into billions of subatomic particles.

<u>Image of the Cyclopzorgs</u>
These are the aliens that used to inhabit the planet Ocat. They are the ones who are threatening other planets such as Xulud and Esile. They have bear and giraffe features, are huge and look very sinister. They are surrounded by high tech equipment.

CYCLOPZORGS OR HUMANS?

Then, just as quickly, they materialized in a room filled with people. That's right, people. These were normal humans. Men and women like the ones in Earth. It took a while for Omsoc and Etnorb to accept what they were seeing. The room was very large and brightly lit with familiar lights. The furniture and everything in the room appeared the same as what one would find back on Earth. The language was the same. There was no need for Athinkobator's Language Universal Translator (LUT). They all seemed very friendly. Omsoc and Etnorb were more than confused; they were bewildered. This was nothing like what they expected to see on this planet. People were going about behaving like anyone would be doing back on Earth.

Omsoc looked at Etnorb and said, "Could this be a trick of some kind? Are we in the right place?"

Etnorb could offer no logical answer to these very valid questions. "Perhaps we should check this with Athinkobator," said Omsoc.

Just as they were about to send a message to Athinkobator, a tall, thin man, who seemed somewhat more distinguished than the others, approached them. He was curious to know who they were and from where they had come. "Welcome," he said in a nonthreatening voice. "What are your names, and where are you from?"

"We are Omsoc and Etnorb from the planet Earth," said Omsoc. "We are here as ambassadors representing the planets Xulud and Esile. We would like to speak with your leader, please?" There was some hesitation to respond by this stranger, and Omsoc and Etnorb became a bit uneasy despite the familiar surroundings, which reminded them of home.

Image of humans in a bar

Omsoc and Etnorb are confused by what they see. On a wall in the background are faded images of Cyclopzorgs (bear and giraffe like features).

What they see are humans. There a many of them in this bar.

All drinking and eating as if they were in any room on Earth.

SAL DEL GOWANBRAE AND DOC DEL PRESTON

The tall, thin man then introduced himself. "I am Sal del Gowanbrae," he said. "We don't get many strangers here. You have obviously come a very long way, and you must have a good reason for doing so. You will come with me. I will take you to the one who will be very interested in what you have told me."

By this time, all eyes in the room were on Omsoc and Etnorb, but they could not understand how it was possible that humans were living on a planet way on the other side of the known universe. This all seemed impossible to comprehend. How did they get here? When did they get here? Were these the Cyclopzorg race? If they were, they certainly looked nothing like how Athinkobator had described them with bear- and giraffe-like features. They were consumed by these thoughts.

As they followed Sal del Gowanbrae, Omsoc leaned towards Etnorb and said, "I think we should first get answers to the questions that are bothering us before we even approach the subject of the Cyclopzorgs."

"Yes," said Etnorb, "this mystery of the humans on planet Ocat is just too important to ignore."

Sal del Gowanbrae escorted Omsoc and Etnorb into another room in which many people were seated in a relaxed manner. In a large chair, in the centre of the room, sat an unshaven man enjoying what looked like homemade slices of meat that looked and smelled like salami. He was also sipping an iridescent green liquid from a tall glass jar, which he held in his left hand. On each side of him stood two very large men with arms crossed and a look of foreboding in their eyes. It was this man to whom Omsoc and Etnorb were brought forward to confront. "Pardon me sir," said Sal del Gowanbrae. "I have two strangers here who claim they are from the remote planet Earth. I think it might be wise for you to speak with them." Sal del

Gowanbrae stepped back and summoned Omsoc and Etnorb to approach.

"I am Doc del Preston," he said. "I am the appointed leader of the people of planet Ocat. I heard about your arrival and something about your intentions. You certainly have gone to a lot of trouble to get here, and I commend you for this. We of the planet Ocat do not normally allow visitors from other worlds for reasons of security and privacy. This planet has a very long history based upon an evolutionary process that exemplifies tyranny, acquisition, and learning. What you see before you is the end result of what was once a race that was motivated by the grandeur of power. I have allowed your starships to enter our world only because of your good intentions, which I was able to establish through our special sensors, which are able to monitor all extraneous activity approaching our world. I liked what I heard about you two. Besides, I think it's about time that some ancient truths about planet Ocat were made known to those that can be trusted. Now, ask your questions."

The open invitation was quite a surprise to both Omsoc and Etnorb. They expected resistance, yet they received the promise of a welcoming transparency from this leader. They wasted no time.

Image of Sal del Gowanbrae & Doc del Preston
Omsoc and Etnorb talk with both these men (they are human).
Sal del Gowanbrae is tall and thin.
In a large armchair, in the centre of the room, sits Doc del Preston;
an unshaven man enjoying what looks like homemade slices
of meat that look and smell like salami. He is also sipping an
irradescent green liquid from a tall glass jar which he holds in his
left hand. He is the leader of the people of planet Ocat.
On each side of him stand two very large men with
arms crossed and a look of foreboding in their eyes.

THE CYCLOPZORG MYSTERY

Omsoc quickly said, "Sir, we have come a long way, as you know, all the way from planet Earth." Doc del Preston nodded as he took another long sip from his glass.

"We do not understand how it's possible that humans are living on this planet," added Etnorb. "Our information tells us that a race of Cyclopzorgs lives here and that they are threatening to change the lives of those living on the planets Xulud and Esile, to change their way of living so that it can be like theirs. We spent much time with the inhabitants of those planets explaining to them that they have every right to live as they wish and to not be afraid to uphold this right against anyone who intends to deny them this privilege. What do you know about the Cyclopzorgs, sir?"

These were certainly valid questions, but whether Omsoc and Etnorb were going to get the answers they wanted or not now became the bigger question. More than ever, they now realized that before they could solve the initial mystery of the Cyclopzorg race, they had to clarify the existence of what seemed like an extension of the human race right here on planet Ocat—a planet that was supposedly inhabited by the Cyclopzorgs.

It took a while for Doc del Preston to respond, and when he did, the answer shocked both Omsoc and Etnorb. "We are humans just like the people on your planet Earth." This answer shook Omsoc and Etnorb from head to toe. They stood transfixed as they waited with bated breath for more of what this leader had to say.

Doc del Preston continued, "More than two thousand of your Earth years ago, a group of Earth people was transported to this planet by an alien race. The earthlings were given no choice. The technology this race had was far beyond anything Earth people had ever seen. They arrived in starships the size of cities. They did not land.

Instead, they hovered in the sky while the onboard supercomputers carried out an analysis of groups of Earth people subjecting them to a series of predetermined tests to establish their suitability for transport to planet Ocat and for subsequent assimilation on that planet. That group of people, which numbered 1,100,999, was brought here at first to see how they would adapt to living on a different world. If the plan worked, they would be forced to stay on the planet with the intention of promulgating a new species—a new, more powerful race. They were not given any special advantages. They had to do the best they could to survive using their own ingenuity." Omsoc and Etnorb were grappling to understand all this.

"Periodic scientific experiments were carried out on every one of these humans. The resulting data was collected and ultimately used to establish how they were adapting to their new environment. It was the Cyclopzorg race that brought those Earth people here." He hesitated to take another drink.

"But where are the Cyclopzorgs? We see no evidence of them anywhere. All we see are humans, at least we think you are still human," asked Omsoc. "There are two planets out there whose inhabitants have been fearful of a Cyclopzorg takeover for centuries. What is going on here?"

Doc del Preston seemed a bit uneasy about this line of questioning. However, Omsoc and Etnorb were determined to remain tenacious until they got the answers they wanted. They owed as much to the people on Xulud and Esile.

"I will answer you," said Doc del Preston, "but this revelation might shock you even further. After many years of attempted integration of these humans by the Cyclopzorgs, something very strange began to happen. The Cyclopzorgs themselves started to become affected by something that they could not have anticipated, let alone understand. In their efforts to diagnose the physiological makeup of these poor humans and to then assimilate them within their own culture, their own lymphatic nodes became infected."

"Are you trying to tell us that the humans infected the Cyclopzorgs?" asked Etnorb.

"That's exactly what I'm saying," said Doc del Preston. "It was only a matter of time before the entire Cyclopzorg race vanished into oblivion. Unbeknownst to them, they had inadvertently introduced to their planet something more than just people of the human race. In a plan that defied any possibility of human understanding at a time of human evolution when science was more fiction than fact, there were certain elements of human physiology which exhibited mechanical, physical, and biochemical functions that could mutate and destroy a foreign symbiotic host. The prolonged association between the different organisms of these two very different species, humans and Cyclopzorgs, did not benefit each other. The human gene acted like an aggressive parasite on the Cyclopzorg physiology. They were eventually destroyed by the very thing that sustains human life and to which the Cyclopzorgs had no resistance." Doc del Preston eased back into his chair and watched as Omsoc and Etnorb tried to understand what they had just heard. There was no denying that this revelation of the Cyclopzorg weakness would come as a shock to anyone who had always thought of that race as formidable and almost indestructible beings.

"Their immune system failed them," said Etnorb in disbelief.

"Yes, that's right," said Doc del Preston. "They were an ugly race, as you already know, but they were extremely intelligent."

Omsoc and Etnorb found this all very incredible and could not believe what they were hearing, but it all seemed to make sense. "Please continue," they said.

"They built these special enclosures for us so that we could survive in this harsh world of theirs," added Doc del Preston. "Everything that we need is available to us in here. Yes, they wanted to change the way of living of the inhabitants of Xulud and Esile, as they had done for many other worlds. They threatened this for thousands of years. We humans tried to convince them not to do this, but they would not listen to us. As the Cyclopzorg race began to diminish in numbers, the real threat to the other planets faded. But because we humans had by now settled well on this planet and wanted to retain our isolation and not be bothered by any other alien race, we kept the threat going. The planets of Xulud and Esile, obviously, have no idea that humans live here on Ocat. They still think it's the Cyclopzorgs occupying this planet. We don't want to change anyone else's way of living. At the same time, we want to be left alone. Can you both understand what I am saying?"

Omsoc and Etnorb were understandably amazed at this revelation. "Mr. Doc del Preston," said Etnorb, "I think I understand. You say that you appreciate the benefits of your people living the lives they wish to live while at the same time allowing the people of other worlds to do the same. Yet, you have allowed the inhabitants of other planets to be afraid of you; well, of the Zorgoncyclops who haven't existed for hundreds of years." There was silence for what seemed a very long time. "This was the wrong thing to do," said Omsoc at last. "You and everyone on Ocat have behaved in the same threatening way as the Zorgoncyclops did when they still controlled this planet. You say you want to be left alone; in your mind, is the only way to do this by instilling fear?" Again there was silence. Both Omsoc and Etnorb could sense an uncomfortable tension building in the room. Were they stretching their welcome? They had no weapons with which to defend themselves if the need arose, but, they knew that Athinkobator was monitoring everything and that it could provide defence capabilities as a last resort. They watched Doc del Preston as he gave them a steely gaze. Finally he spoke. "How dare you come here from Earth to confront me with your goodwill intentions," he muttered. Earth people have a lot to answer for and in some ways, I have to say that it was probably not such a bad thing that our ancestors were taken here by the Zorgoncyclops so long ago. At least we have learned to live in peace among ourselves." "Of course you are right," said Etnorb. "We did not come here to create any disharmony. We had no idea what to expect from the Zorgoncyclops; we certainly did not expect to find humans living on this planet. Can't there be a sharing of cultures, which will enrich your world of Ocat as well as the worlds of Xulud and Esile."

"This is the main reason why we have travelled across the universe," continued Omsoc. "We totally believe in equality among the various races of different worlds, and we want to spread this message of equality and how it can benefit everyone as far across the vastness of space as possible, even to worlds yet unknown." Omsoc and Etnorb were starting to feel uneasy again; so much depended on the success of their mission. The inhabitants of two worlds were living in fear of having their lives disrupted. Perhaps other worlds would also face this same fear in the future. They knew that they must not fail.

"I am still not convinced," said Doc del Preston as he took another long drink from his glass. "What guarantee do I have that if the true nature of the inhabitants of Ocat are revealed to the planets Xulud and Esile and to others, that we here on ocat won't eventually be faced with the same threat?" This was a good point that was raised and Omsoc and Etnorb knew that the right response had to be given. "Doc del preston," said Etnorb. "On our long journey to your plaet, we visited the planet Barbabeetle. On that planet, we had the great honour to meet with the planet's leader, Onigiul. He allowed us the rare privilege to have an audience with the very wise Ecarg. Surely, a person in your position will have heard of Ecarg?" Doc del Preston appeared to be somewhat astounded by what Etnorb had just said. "Of course I have heard of the great Ecarg of the planet Barbabeetle," he quickly replied. "But, I thought that it was all stuff of mythology; fantastic, but not real." "It's real alright and Omsoc will confirm this as will the two starship warrior captains, Emo-Demo and Majac, who brought us there. The wise Ecarg gave us guidelines and promise of support to assist us in our quest for peace between your world and the other worlds. If I said to you that the great Ecarg will oversee the peace process for all worlds, would you and your people be prepared to openly declare your true identity?" Doc del Preston was very impressed upon hearing of the wise Ecarg. "If what you say is all true," he said, "Then I have no hesitation to do what you ask."

"Do you think that Etnorb and I could come back when you're ready so that we can help the people of Ocat, Xulud, and Esile achieve something really special by sharing their lives and their knowledge freely," added Omsoc.

Doc del Preston was more than happy for this to happen and promised not to send any more threats to the worlds of Xulud and Esile. He decreed this new policy in a direct order to all the inhabitants of planet Ocat.

RETURN TO XULUD AND ESILE

O msoc and Etnorb were now ready to be transported back to their starships, where Emo-Demo and Majac were waiting to take them back to the planets Xulud and Esile. They were very pleased with the way things had turned out, and they were eager to deliver the good news to the leaders of those planets, Grayluke and Queen Becca.

"I still can't believe what has just happened," said Etnorb. "Who would have ever thought that there would be humans living on Ocat—a planet so far outside of the limits of the known universe."

Omsoc replied in a humbled tone of voice, "There are so many unknowns in the universe. You should know that, Etnorb. We have only just started to scratch the surface of what is yet to be discovered out there. Remember, there are as many, if not more, star systems out there than there are grains of sand on all the beaches on Earth."

"The wonders of nature and science never cease to amaze me," said Etnorb. A quick signal to Athinkobator back on Earth, and they were instantly beamed from their position in the building and back on board their respective starships. The pilots had already mapped the return journey using complicated astrometric computer programming, which combined Athinkobator's computer core array with that of the starships' onboard computer systems. At the instant the coordinates were punched in, the starships zipped into the wormhole; and in a fraction of a second, they were on the planets Xulud and Esile.

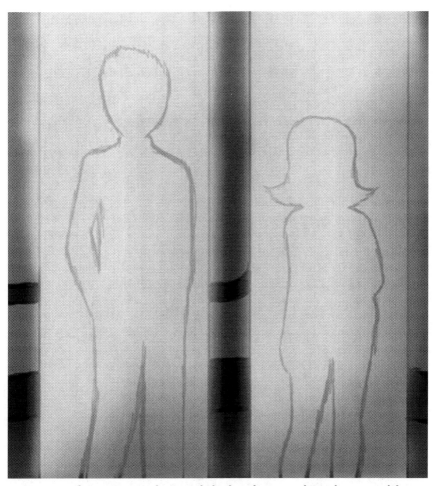

Image of Omsoc and Etnorb being beamed to the starships Kert1701 and JJ57

Omsoc and Etnorb are beamed from their position in the bar to their respective starships (Omsoc to Kert1701 and Etnorb to JJ57). They are dematerialized in the bar room and transported to the starships where they re-materialize. The pilots are in the spaceships (X-Mankane is in Kert1701 and Majac is in JJ57)

Omsoc and Etnorb were soon talking to the leaders, Grayluke and Queen Becca. They explained to them that planet Ocat would no longer be a threat to their worlds as they were able to reach a mutual understanding of the importance of peace and harmony between the worlds, with the leader, Doc del Preston. "It might seem quite incredible," said Omsoc to Grayluke. "But, it's true. "You and all the Sebemos now need not be afraid anymore." Etnorb was on the planet Esile. She sat with Queen Becca and some of her guards but wasn't sure what she should tell her. "First, I want to let you know that all went well on the planet Ocat," she said. "From now on, the Gubeiggas will be able to live the life that they want. You will not be attacked by the Zorgoncyclops." This important news was quickly relayed to everyone on the planets Xulud and Esile. After hearing the news, the Sebemos on Xulud and the Gubeiggas on Esile were very happy and relieved that their lives were not going to be forcibly changed. It was Grayluke who first questioned them about the Cyclopzorgs. "Why did they change their mind so quickly?" He asked. "I would also like to know more," added Queen Becca. "Surely there must have been some very difficult discussions between you and them?"

Both Grayluke and Queen Becca remained linked through the huge video screens and all the inhabitants of both planets watched and waited for Omsoc and Etnorb to answer. Omsoc was the first to say something. "What I am about to tell you will both shock and surprise you. There were no Zorgoncyclops." Grayluke and Queen Becca couldn't believe what they had just heard. Was this a joke? How could these two intrepid space travelers make such a statement? The threats that the planets Xulud and Esile had been exposed to for countless years were had been very real. If this was an attempt at humour by Omsoc and etnorb, then it was in very poor taste. "What are you saying," asked Grayluke. "Look, I know that you are finding this hard to believe," added Etnorb, "but, what Omsoc is saying is the truth. We arrived on the planet Ocat fully expecting a confrontation with the evil Zorgoncyclops. We were just as surprised as you are now when we discovered that they do not exist anymore. In fact, they haven't been around for hundreds of years." The planetary leaders, Grayluke and Queen Becca, were understandably confused. "Well, if it hasn't been the Zorgoncyclops that have been causing us grief, who was it then?" asked Queen Becca. "Brace yourselves," said Omsoc, "because you're not going to believe what I am going to tell you. It was human beings."

Both Grayluke and Queen Becca reeled in disbelief. They couldn't possibly understand this. Their home worlds had been placed under threat by the very same people that they had asked to help them. It just didn't seem possible. Omsoc and Etnorb almost regretted having told them the truth, but, they knew that it was the best thing to do. They were young, but, they knew how it felt when kids their own age played tricks on them by withholding the truth about important things. They always felt betrayed. An explanation was needed now and fast. "We can explain everything," said Omsoc. It took some time, but, once they had finished, they could see that there was understanding from the planetary leaders Grayluke and Queen Becca. Their ambassadors, X-Mankane and Aggie-Bug also expressed understanding.

**Image of Omsoc now on planet Xulud
and Etnorb on planet Esile**

Omsoc (on planet Xulud) and Etnorb (on planet Esile) relaying
the good news to the respective leaders of the planets
(Grayluke and Queen Becca). Grayluke is the leader of the
Sebemo race and Queen Becca is the leader of the Gubeigga
race).........the Sebemo look like the computer chip and the
Gubeigga look almost human, with a pointy head and wings.

BACK TO EARTH

I t was time for Omsoc and Etnorb to now return to Earth and to enter all the data that they had collected of their adventure into Athinkobator's vast memory banks. Commanders Emo-Demo and Majac were ready with their starships. X-Mankane and Aggie-Bug also thanked Omsoc and Etnorb on behalf of their leaders, Grayluke and Queen Becca, and also on behalf of their people. Omsoc and Etnorb suited up and looked at each other before they entered their starships.

"This has been a most amazing journey," said Omsoc. "The experience has been out of this world," said Etnorb as they both shook hands.

"I wonder if our friends back on Earth will believe what we have been through. From that moment when Athinkobator was first activated by those unusual energy beams, it has been one surprise after another."

Etnorb looked at Omsoc with mixed feelings of disappointment and excitement. "You know," said Etnorb, "it is sad that it's all over, but I'm glad that we achieved something very positive for the inhabitants of Xulud and Esile, and in some way, for those on Ocat also."

Omsoc agreed, saying, "We really make a good team. Let's get on board our starships. Commanders Emo-Demo and Majac are waiting to take us back to Earth."

Once Omsoc and Etnorb were on board and enclosed in their trans-space transporter tubes; the crack pilots expertly manoeuvered their ships into the wormhole, and in the blink of an eye, they were back on Earth in front of Athinkobator.

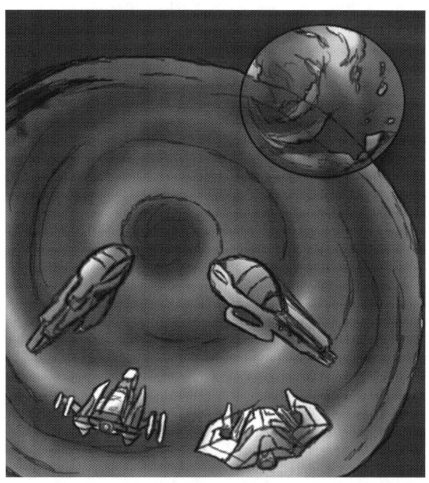

Image of Commanders Emo-Demo and Majac in their starships
Omsoc and Etnorb are now with them. A massive wormhole
forms. Earth is in the distance. Starship Kert1701 is on
the bottom left and starship jj57 is bottom right.

"You know what," said Omsoc, "I'm afraid to check, but do you remember that when we left on our journey, we were travelling on time as it related to 'ship' time? This meant a big inconsistency between clock time on board the starships and Earth time. According to onboard ship time, we have only been away for 24.365 days."

"That's right," reflected Etnorb. "But 24,365 years have elapsed here on Earth. Does this mean that anybody we knew before we started our journey does not exist now? Could it possibly mean that nobody now even knows that we were on a journey of peace, that we have come back to a world that is totally foreign to us?"

It was then that Athinkobator gave them their answer. "Do not be concerned," it said. "Thanks to the curvature of space and the time-warp continuum that I have been controlling since your departure, you are back in present-day real time." There was great relief on their faces upon hearing this. They all disembarked. The secret compound was filled with important officials who were waiting to welcome back the two travelers who had represented Earth so well. The news of their success had preceded them, thanks to

Athinkobator. It had informed them all about Omsoc's and Etnorb's volunteer mission and the successful outcome. The leaders of every country were there to congratulate them and to extend to them their country's highest honours. This was a proud moment indeed for all concerned.

Image of Omsoc and Etnorb surrounded by the leaders of Earth
The image shows Omsoc and Etnorb being congratulated
by the leaders of Earth (Generals etc). They are
standing in front of the Athinkobator computer.

Omsoc and Etnorb took some time to come back into their own reality on Earth. "Did you expect any of this?" Etnorb asked Omsoc.

"I did not," answered Omsoc, "but I'm pleased."

The starship commanders, Emo-Demo and Majac, were still there with them, ready to return to their own worlds of Xulud and Esile. They stood to attention and smartly saluted Omsoc and Etnorb as a sign of respect and appreciation for all they had done to help their people.

"Why don't you stay with us for a while?" asked Etnorb. "The people of Earth will want to meet you. We can learn so much from each other." Emo-Demo and Majac were flattered by the invitation, but they knew that they had to return to their own worlds.

"Perhaps there will be another time," said Majac.

"We appreciate your offer," said Emo-Demo. "But we have to return to our own planets. There is much to be done." They then climbed back into their starships and prepared all systems for their return journeys home. Athinkobator reactivated the wormhole as the starships positioned themselves automatically within their respective energy beams. Commanders Emo-Demo and Majac punched their home coordinates into their onboard computers, and the starships entered the wormhole. There was a momentary flash of bright light, and the wormhole collapsed within itself, hurtling the two starships back to Xulud and Esile at the speed of thought.

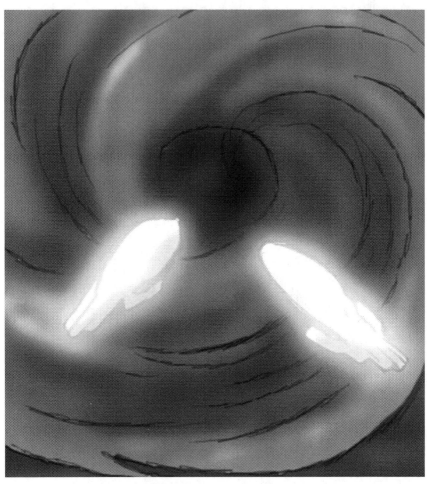

<u>Image of X-Mankane and Majac starships</u>
<u>preparing to return home</u>

They are in their starships. Athinkobator re-activates the
wormhole. There is a flash of light and the ships are gone.

"I still find all this hard to believe," said Etnorb. "So much has happened, and now that it's all done, I feel that I could do it all over again—relive the adventure as it were. Do you feel the same urge that I do, Omsoc?"

"I do, but don't worry, I get the feeling that somehow, there will be other adventures lurking somewhere and just waiting to engage us."

"I suppose you're right," said Etnorb. "I hope so anyway. In the meantime, we can always think about what we have been through and how we have been able to help others. Thanks to the amazing technology that is Athinkobator."

"One thing that I will always have difficulty coming to grips with," said Omsoc, "is what happened on planet Ocat. We didn't see any Cyclopzorgs, and I'm thankful for that, but what about the human population that lives there? They are descendants of people of our own kind that were transported there, taken away from their homes and their own families thousands of years ago."

Etnorb thought about what Omsoc had just said, and the reply he gave shocked even Omsoc. "Yes, that was wrong. Now that we know what is possible, I suspect that even at this very moment, we could be under the watchful eye of some alien power just waiting to make contact in some way. Let's hope that they are friendly. But I take comfort from the fact that we have the unbeatable computer power of Athinkobator. Nothing will be able to surpass its ability in providing Earth with unlimited protection."

"Don't forget, Etnorb, we now also have some very good allies from four worlds—Barbabeetle, Xulud, Esile, and Ocat."

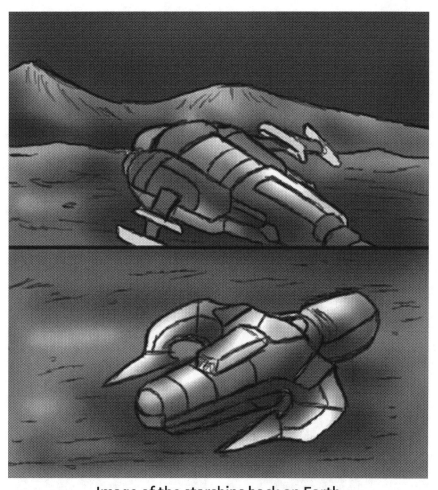

<u>Image of the starships back on Earth</u>
The image should show the starships outside the
huge underground compound where Athinkobator
computer is secretely hidden. Starship Kert1701
is on the top and starship jj57 is bottom.

Omsoc and Etnorb are checking time scales. They are comparing Earth time with ship time with the Athinkobator computer.

Image of Omsoc and Etnorb & Athinkobator
The image is of Omsoc and Etnorb sitting in front of
Athinkobator's large control panel. From the screen
are projections of the worlds BARBABEETLE, XULUD,
ESILE & OCAT. These worlds appear to be streaming
out of the large screen each enveloped in its own energy
beam above the heads of Omsoc and Etnorb.

DID IT REALLY HAPPEN?

After all the celebrations had ended, Omsoc and Etnorb sat at Athinkobator's big control panel to review their experience. Only then did they discover that Athinkobator had recorded their entire journey within the circuitry of its limitless holographic virtual reality—a reality so intense and so probable that it's storage matrix or data base could generate any given or imagined dimensions. "We have been transported through and have experienced what it's like in four-dimensional space-time," said Omsoc. "Don't forget how the passing of time at faster than light speed affected the space-time continuum. We got dragged into four-dimensional space-time," said Etnorb. "I think that Athinkobator somehow has managed to transcend all known laws of mathematical probability? It has been able to compute beyond the special theory of relativity, unifying electromagnetism with gravity in a five-dimensional configuration," said Omsoc. "Maybe Athinkobator has expanded its computing ability to a new generation of quantum physics efficiency," continued Etnorb. "This scares me."

"We have been drawn into an adventure of such unimaginable proportions by Athinkobator itself," said Omsoc.

That was correct. Everything they had done was being vividly replayed to them on Athinkobator's huge multifaceted, three-dimensional plasma screen; Athinkobator was making it happen all over again. They looked at the passage of time that had elapsed since the start of their journey on the chronometer indicator on the panel. Only seconds had gone by since the first energy beam had appeared to them. If Athinkobator was able to restore time, as had just happened, what else could it do? Did they dare ask this question of Athinkobator? Of course they did. What kid would want to miss out on another adventure of a lifetime?

"Athinkobator," commanded Omsoc, "we wish to remain in the image of our alter egos. Capture our previous identities and encrypt-program them into your memory core in a repeat loop format. This status is to remain until a certain condition, predetermined by us, is satisfied. We will now program this condition as an end statement in the loop program. Note that this is not an infinity loop. Now, before the loop is started, demonstrate to us once more who we really are." In that instant, Athinkobator transformed the appearance of the entire complex they were occupying. The setting became a scene going back to a time of almost five years in the past. The location was familiar to them. The main building had a steeple and a cross, and there was a statue. Seconds later, Athinkobator activated its central processing unit and immediately locked this scene, including the characters of that time, in a reality loop that would exist only in the vast recesses of Athinkobator's myriad array of circuitry.

<u>Image of Cosmo and Bronte & Athinkobator</u>
The image should be of Cosmo & Bronte as the dog and the cat
(not there alter egos). They are surrounded by the characters
from the previous story book (The Secret At St Mary's)

THE END (OR IS IT)?

Omsoc and Etnorb didn't take long to realize that their mission, apart from it being a success and an amazing experience, had also expanded Athinkobator's positronic circuitry beyond any expectations. "Athinkobator," commanded Omsoc and Etnorb together, "this is now our new reality." They both stood motionless in the room for just a few seconds before they quickly and expertly took their places at Athinkobator's large range of controls.

They were back at Athinkobator's screen as the superheroes Omsoc and Etnorb. "You know something," said Omsoc. "I already miss being on an adventure." It didn't take Etnorb long to reply. "I wonder if Athinkobator is capable of creating simulations of any kind. What if it can create realities for us to experience without even having to leave this place?" "I've heard that there are such mysteries as parallel universes," said Omsoc. "Imagine being able to visit a universe just like ours where there are worlds also colliding; where things are happening just like they are here but on a scale a hundred times bigger?" These ideas did seem a bit preposterous, but, they knew they had to find out. All they had to do was enter Athinkobator's Techtronic Simulator Conversion Capsules and instruct Athinkobator as to what they wanted to experience. As they were about to do this, there suddenly appeared, on their screens, words they had never before seen or heard, NERAK . . . MAS . . Ycnan . . . SIRK . . . ONNON . . . ECARG . . . ENAJASIL . . . Was this a message in code coming to them from some point in hyperspace; from some distant star system; perhaps even from a parallel universe; or was Athinkobator just setting up for a new adventure? It was almost as if Athinkobator had read their minds. Didn't matter. "I'm prepared," said Omsoc. "What about you?" Etnorb was now prepared for anything that Athinkobator could come up with from the deep recesses of its limitless power. All they had to do was give the command.

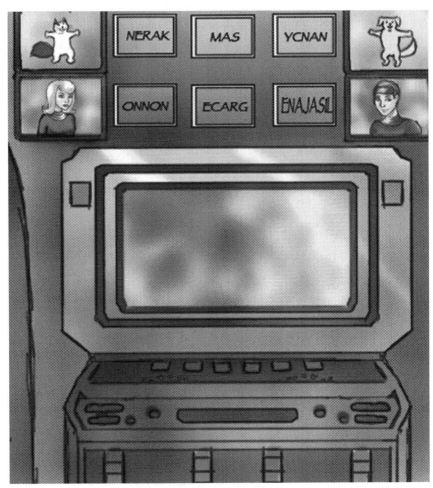

Image of Athinkobator

The image is of Athinkobator. It's main screen shows the images of Cosmo the dog, Bronte the cat, Omsoc and Etnorb. The image also shows 6 other minor screens. Each screen shows one of the following images:-

NERAK................. MAS.................... YCNAN...................
ONNON...........................ECARG.....................ENAJASIL

"We have at our disposal the most powerful and complex machine that has ever been created," said Etnorb. "Nobody really knows all that it might be capable of doing. Just imagine what our friends at school would think if they knew about Athinkobator and what we have just experienced."

Omsoc and Etnorb immediately decided that it was their duty, their responsibility to the scientific world and to all mankind, indeed to all creatures of the universe, that they discover the full potential of Athinkobator. Perhaps they would test its ability to travel beyond the fourth and fifth dimensions, such as nonlinear time, which would provide a window into other dimensions yet unheard of. Perhaps they could discover parallel worlds and maybe even parallel galaxies. Only time would tell. One thing is for certain, however, Omsoc and Etnorb have again succeeded in proving that anything is possible if one believes that it is.

"As we grow, we are told that the world is what it is, and we have to live within it," said Etnorb. "But it can be said that everything around us was created by people no smarter than you or I, Omsoc, so *you* or *I* or any of our friends can change it."

Like Omsoc and Etnorb, if *you* are crazy enough to try to change the world for the better, then, *you* are the one who will most likely do so. Never stop looking for what's not there. After all, isn't it true that things that can occur will occur in our faraway inner world?